Timmy and his godparents, Cosmo and Wanda, watched the Valentine's ___ in Fairyland.

"I didn't realize Valentine's Day was such a big deal ove___

Suddenly Cupid appeared. "Valentine's love is the most p___ ___ ___ there is!" he declared.

"Tomorrow I've got to make as many people as possible fall in love so I can retain my powers," continued Cupid. "And I've got an arrow with your name on it!"

"You mean Trixie Tang will finally fall in love with me?" Timmy asked eagerly.

Cupid frowned. "I was thinking of your baby-sitter Vicky's little sister."

"NOT TOOTIE!" screamed Timmy.

LOVESTRUCK!

BY DAVID LEWMAN   ILLUSTRATED BY JASON FRUCHTER
BASED ON THE TELEPLAY BY BUTCH HARTMAN, STEVE MARMEL, AND SCOTT FELLOWS

SCHOLASTIC INC.

New York Toronto London Auckland Sydney
Mexico City New Delhi Hong Kong Buenos Aires

The next day was Valentine's Day, and Timmy tried his best to impress Trixie. But she completely rejected him.

"At least no one saw her turn me down," muttered Timmy.

"HA HA HA HA HA HA HA!"

Timmy whirled around and saw every girl in Dimmsdale laughing at him! "Who'd want to be *his* Valentine?" jeered one of the girls.

"*I* would!" said Tootie, running up with candy and flowers. "I think he's dreamy!" Timmy ran from the girls as fast as he could. "Get all the girls away from me! I wish I lived in a world without girls!" he pleaded.

Cosmo and Wanda frowned, but they waved their wands and . . . **POOF!**

Timmy's mom was just about to serve a plate of waffles to his dad when . . . **POOF!** She disappeared!

The stack of waffles turned into a football.

Timmy's dad grabbed the football. "Hike! Hike! Hike!"

With a huge **POOF!** a high brick wall appeared, dividing the planet into two halves. On one side of the wall the women and girls appeared one by one. "Ooh, I feel weird," Vicky murmured.

Timmy's mom blinked. "I feel as though we women can finally paint our vision of what the world should be!" she announced.

The girls and women cheered. Ten minutes later they had built a gleaming, towering city called Hersdale.

Shoes

32 floors of

Perfume

NAILS

CHAN
5

GOURMET

"Yay!" cheered Timmy. "All the girls went away!"
Wanda was puzzled. "Wait a minute," she said,
"I'm a girl!"
POOF! She disappeared!
"Wanda?" asked Timmy, looking around.

GONE!

Then ... **POOF!** Timmy and Cosmo suddenly found themselves in a wrestling ring. "What's a Wanda?" asked Cosmo, slightly dazed.

"It's a ... uh ... wrestling move!" Timmy said, covering for Wanda's disappearance. "Like a body slam! WANDA!" Timmy leaped onto Cosmo, knocking him to the mat.

Meanwhile Cupid discovered what was happening.

"AHHHH!" he screamed. "Get my cherubs out there to spread love before we lose all power!"

A squadron of cherubs zoomed toward Earth, but they were too weak to fly.

"Find me the person who's responsible for this mess," Cupid said, groaning.

Back in Dimmsdale every man did whatever he wanted. Nobody realized anything was different . . . except for Cosmo.

"I can't help but think that something's missing," Cosmo said, wondering.

Timmy was having too much fun to wish the world back to normal. "I love it here!" he said.

BURP!

Meanwhile Cupid was getting weaker by the minute. "Any news?" he managed to ask his sergeant.

The officer cleared his throat. "Well, the boys and girls are still magically separated, sir. And you're running out of love power . . . fast." "This is the worst Valentine's Day ever!" cried Cupid.

The sergeant looked at his clipboard. "Don't fret, sir. We'll find out who's responsible."

Cupid coughed and uttered, "If this meter hits Nots O' Love, I'm going to disappear forever . . . and so will love!"

When Timmy got home he found his dad crying. "I can't help but feel that something's missing," said Mr. Turner.

Cosmo was crying too. He missed Wanda without even remembering her.

Realizing he'd made a mistake, Timmy wished the girls were back. But Cosmo couldn't remember what girls were, so he couldn't bring them back!

In Hersdale the girls also felt something was missing.

"Maybe it's waffle irons!" exclaimed Timmy's mom. She pulled one out and cradled it lovingly. "I'll call you 'Dad.'"

Tootie pulled out a dollhouse. "And I'm naming this dollhouse 'Timmy.'"

But then she and Timmy's mom started to cry. The other women cried too.

Timmy and Cosmo decided to knock the brick wall down with a giant steak. "When the boys and girls see each other," said Timmy, "they're bound to remember about love, and then Valentine's Day will be saved!"

The wall crashed down. The two sides stared at each other.

"I'll bet they think they're better than we are," said the boys.

"Should we clean them?" asked Timmy's mom.

"I say we go to war!" shouted Vicky.

"That's a great idea!" said Timmy's dad.

The men and women charged at each other.

"Where's the love?" Timmy screamed.

Timmy was about to be crushed when Cupid sucked him
up through a tiny portal into his Fairyland headquarters.
"That's the one, sir," said the sergeant. "Timmy Turner.
He started this whole mess."

"Cupid!" said Timmy. "You've got to do something!"

"I can't," answered Cupid, weakly. "I don't have enough power left."

"I can help!" exclaimed Timmy.

Cupid's assistants quickly dressed Timmy like a ninja and gave him a love-thrower.

"I'm ready," Timmy said with determination. "Let's get mushy."

Timmy landed in the battlefield. He threw love-filled hearts, and whomever he hit stopped fighting and instantly fell in love.

But Timmy needed help. Now that there was some love, Cupid grew stronger and sent his cherubs down to Earth.

Timmy searched until he found
Wanda and Cosmo, fighting with
their wands. He carefully aimed his
love thrower and pulled the trigger.
They were in love again!

Timmy ran up to them. "I
wish the world was back to
normal!" he blurted out.
POOF!
His wish came true!

To thank Timmy, Cupid let him use his arrow however he wanted to.

Timmy decided that Trixie didn't deserve his love. He walked over to Tootie and stuck Cupid's arrow in his body.

"Tootie, will you be my Valentine?" asked Timmy. Tootie beamed. "Yes! Yes! Yes!" she declared. Cosmo watched Tootie and Timmy holding hands. "Cosmo," said Wanda, "stop looking and kiss me!"